HOW TO TRAIN YOUR DRAGON

THE HIDDEN WORLD

THE NIGHT FURY AND THE LIGHT FURY

Adapted by Tina Gallo
Illustrated by Shane L. Johnson

Ready-to-Read

Simon Spotlight

New York   London   Toronto   Sydney   New Delhi

SIMON SPOTLIGHT

An imprint of Simon & Schuster Children's Publishing Division

1230 Avenue of the Americas, New York, New York 10020

How to Train Your Dragon: The Hidden World © 2019 DreamWorks Animation LLC. All Rights Reserved.

This Simon Spotlight edition January 2019

All rights reserved, including the right of reproduction in whole or in part in any form.

SIMON SPOTLIGHT, READY-TO-READ, and colophon are registered trademarks of Simon & Schuster, Inc.

For information about special discounts for bulk purchases, please contact Simon & Schuster Special Sales at 1-866-506-1949 or business@simonandschuster.com.

Manufactured in the United States of America 0320 LAK

8 10 9 7

ISBN 978-1-5344-3835-4 (hc)

ISBN 978-1-5344-3834-7 (pbk)

ISBN 978-1-5344-3836-1 (eBook)

Toothless was a Night Fury dragon.
Hiccup was a Viking.
They should have been enemies,
but they were best friends.

For many years
Vikings believed dragons
were dangerous and
should be destroyed.
Young Hiccup didn't think like this.

He caught a dragon
he called Toothless.
He tried being friendly instead.
Toothless tried
being friendly, too.

Another time
Hiccup reached out
to pet Toothless.
Toothless loved it.

Against all odds
the Viking and the dragon
became friends.

Hiccup saw that
Toothless was missing a tail fin,
and he could not fly.

Hiccup made a new tail fin
for Toothless.
They became best friends.

Toothless would do anything
to protect Hiccup.
He even battled dragons
much bigger than he was,
and he won!
Toothless became the Alpha
dragon, the leader of all dragons.

Dragons started to live
with the Vikings
on the island of Berk.

One day Toothless heard a groan
in the forest.
He followed the sound, and
found a female dragon
that looked a lot like him.
They understood each other's
caws and expressions.

Toothless did not notice
what was hidden in the clearing.
Get out of here! It's a trap,
she purred to Toothless.
He stepped around the trap
and got closer to her.

Then Hiccup arrived
with his girlfriend, Astrid.
The new dragon was scared.
She shot a violet fireball at them!
Toothless told the white dragon
to stop.
But they're humans! she roared.

She did not trust humans and
flew away.
Toothless roared, *Come back!*
Hiccup and Astrid were amazed.
They realized the dragon was not
a Night Fury—but a *Light Fury*!

Later at the dragon stables
Toothless grew restless.
Hiccup didn't know what
was bothering Toothless.
"Isn't it obvious?" asked Astrid.
"He's in love!"

Hiccup was surprised.
He asked Toothless,
"Am I not enough?"
Toothless paused then dashed
away.

Hiccup was worried.
Someone had tried to lure Toothless
by using the Light Fury to trap him.
Berk was too dangerous
for dragons.
When Hiccup was younger,
his father, Stoick, told him
a story of a Hidden World
guarded by dragons.
The waterfall entrance
led to a land beneath the sea.
Hiccup wanted to find this place.

Soon the Vikings packed and went
to find the Hidden World
with the dragons.
Hiccup and Toothless led the way.
Suddenly, Toothless heard a noise.
It was the Light Fury!

The Light Fury grabbed Hiccup and
tossed him into the ocean.
She showed Toothless he was free.
Toothless smiled,
thanking the Light Fury,
but rushed to save Hiccup.
The confused Light Fury flew away.

The Vikings and dragons continued
their search for the Hidden World.
On the way they found an island
and rested there for the night.
The Light Fury found them.
A happy Toothless followed her.

The Light Fury invited Toothless
to dance with her.
Toothless just flapped his wings.
He didn't know what to do.
Then Toothless got an idea.
He took a twig and drew
in the sand.
He drew the Light Fury!

The Light Fury touched her nose
to Toothless's nose.
She invited him to fly away with her.
He tried to follow her
but fell into the water.
He could not fly without Hiccup.

Hiccup made Toothless a new tail
fin so he could fly on his own.
Toothless met the Light Fury.
They flew off together.
The Light Fury showed Toothless
a giant hole in the ocean.
It was surrounded by waterfalls.

My home, the Light Fury purred
to Toothless.
He sounded back, *Take me there.*
The Light Fury held
one of his talons.
They disappeared into the hole.

Hiccup wondered what happened to Toothless.

He and Astrid flew off on Astrid's Tracker Class dragon to search for Toothless. They found the giant hole in the ocean and flew into it. They saw the Hidden World Hiccup's father had told him about!